A Hat Full of Gold

Written by Lisa Thompson
Pictures by Craig Smith and Lew Keilar

Captain Red Beard was asleep
in his hammock.

He was dreaming
of treasure.

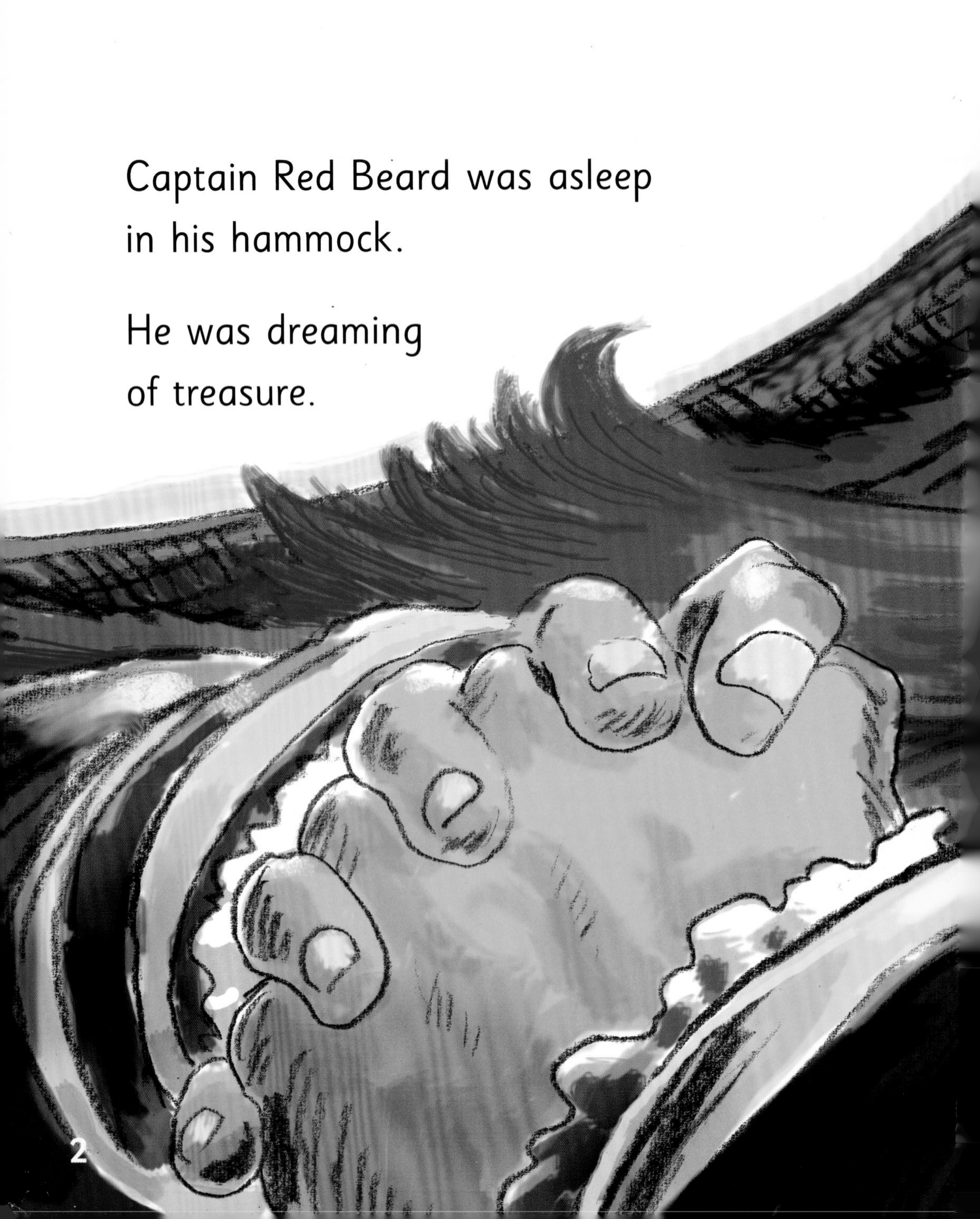

When he woke up he had a strange feeling. Something was missing.

What was it? Fingers, the parrot, was on her perch. Bones, the sea dog, was in the lookout. Lizzie, the first mate, was at the helm.

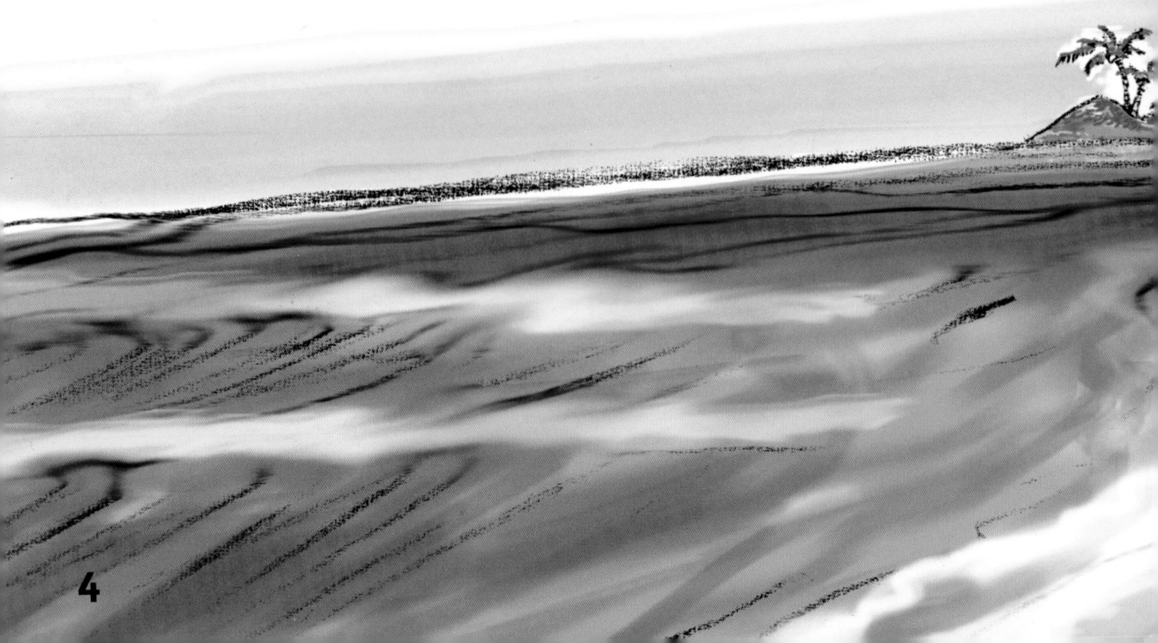

Captain Red Beard scratched his head and patted his hair.

Patting his hair felt strange. He patted it again. Something was missing.

"My hat!" said Captain Red Beard. "My pirate hat is missing!"

Captain Red Beard looked under the hammock.
He looked above the hammock.

He looked right. He looked left.

There was no sign of his hat.

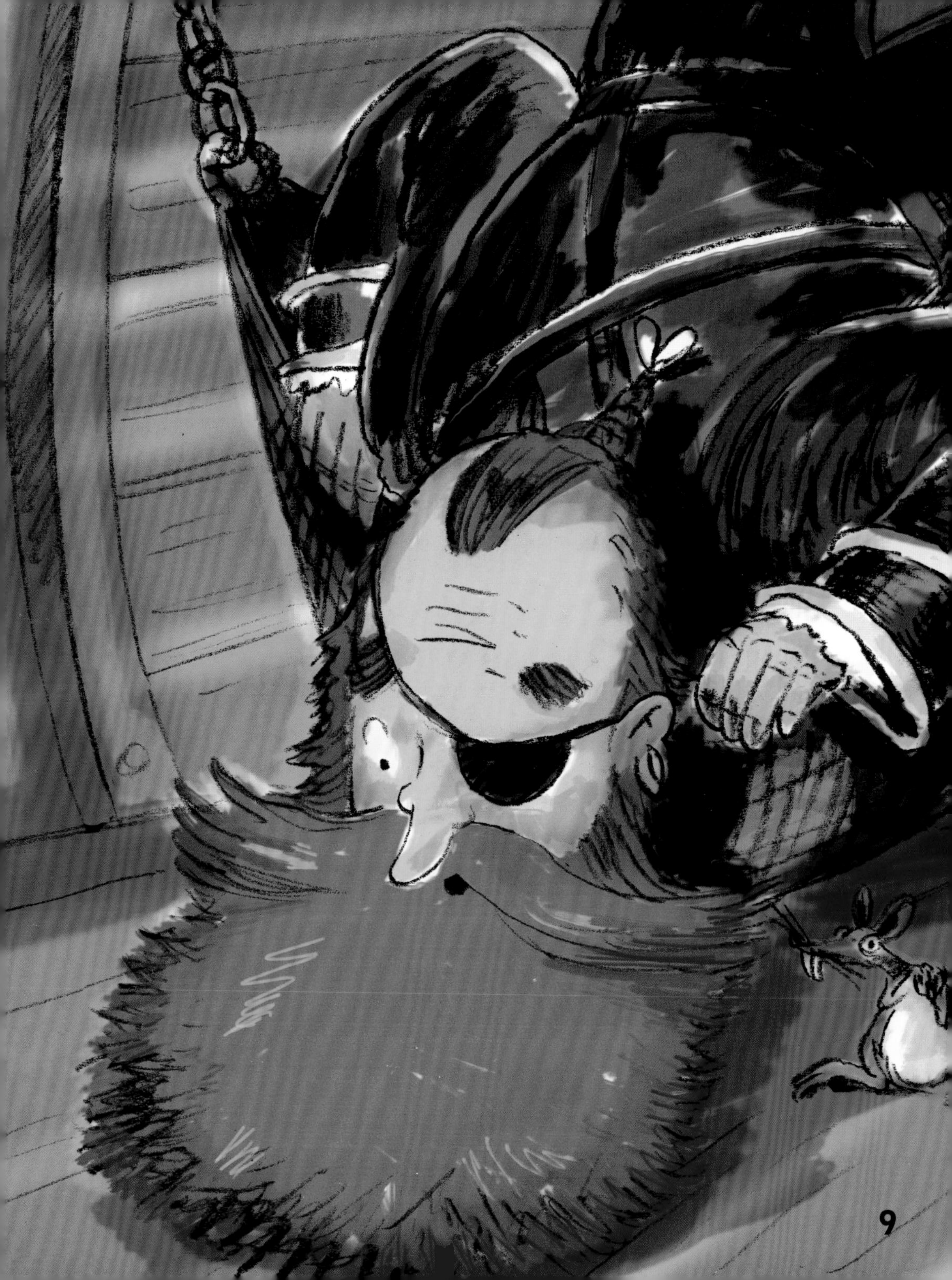

“A hat full of gold for the pirate who finds my hat!” said Captain Red Beard.

“Find it faster than a flying cannonball!”

P.U.
Maps

"Dirty rotten pirates," said Fingers the parrot.

She flew around the ship looking for the hat.
She checked between the sails.

She did not find the Captain's hat,
but she did find her lost packet
of biscuits.

Bones checked inside the boxes,
the barrels and the boats.

He did not find the Captain's hat,
but he did find his
lost scarf.

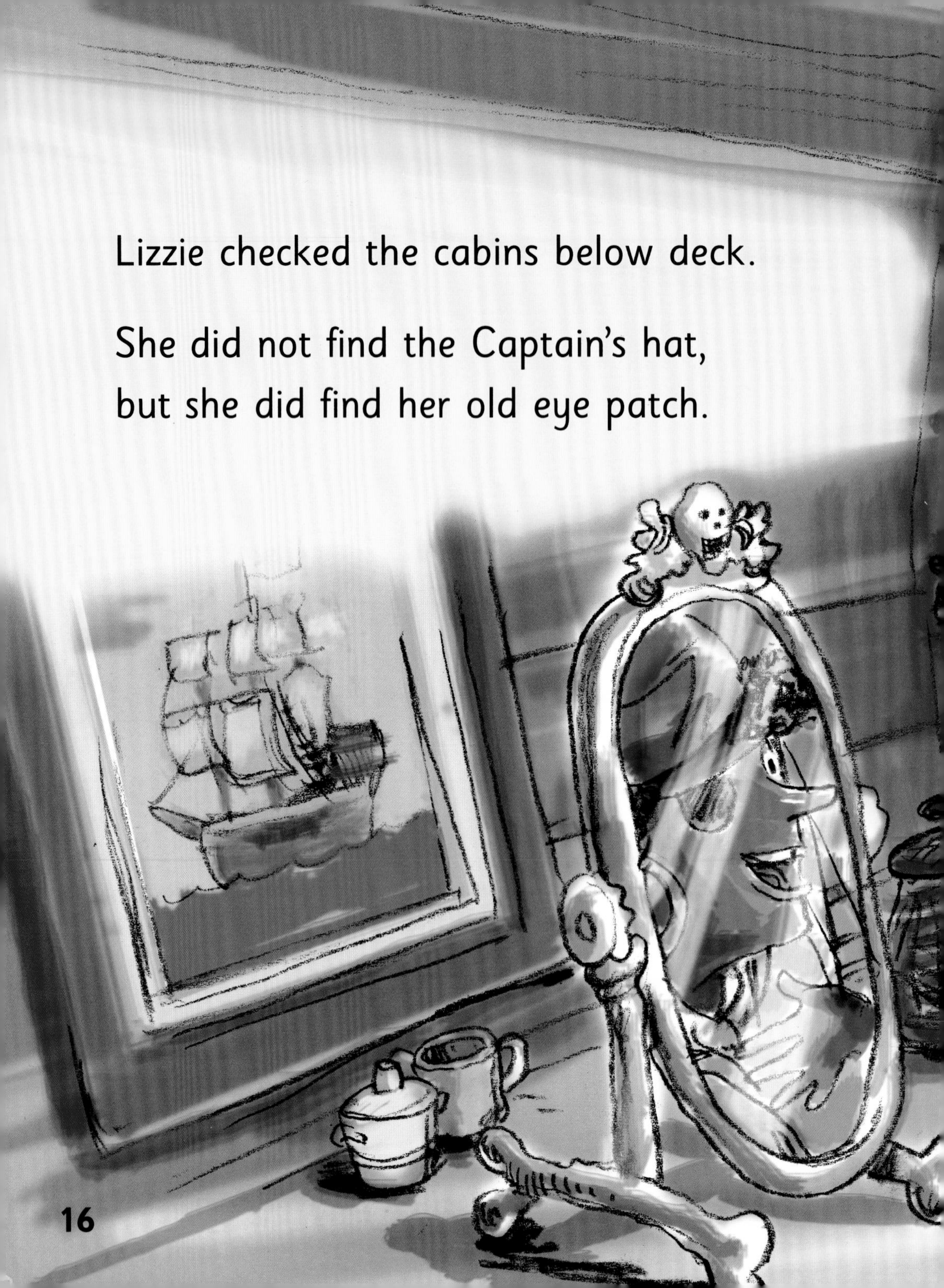

Lizzie checked the cabins below deck.

She did not find the Captain's hat,
but she did find her old eye patch.

"Any sign of my hat?" said the Captain.

"No. We're very sorry, Captain," said the crew.

Captain Red Beard did not look pleased.

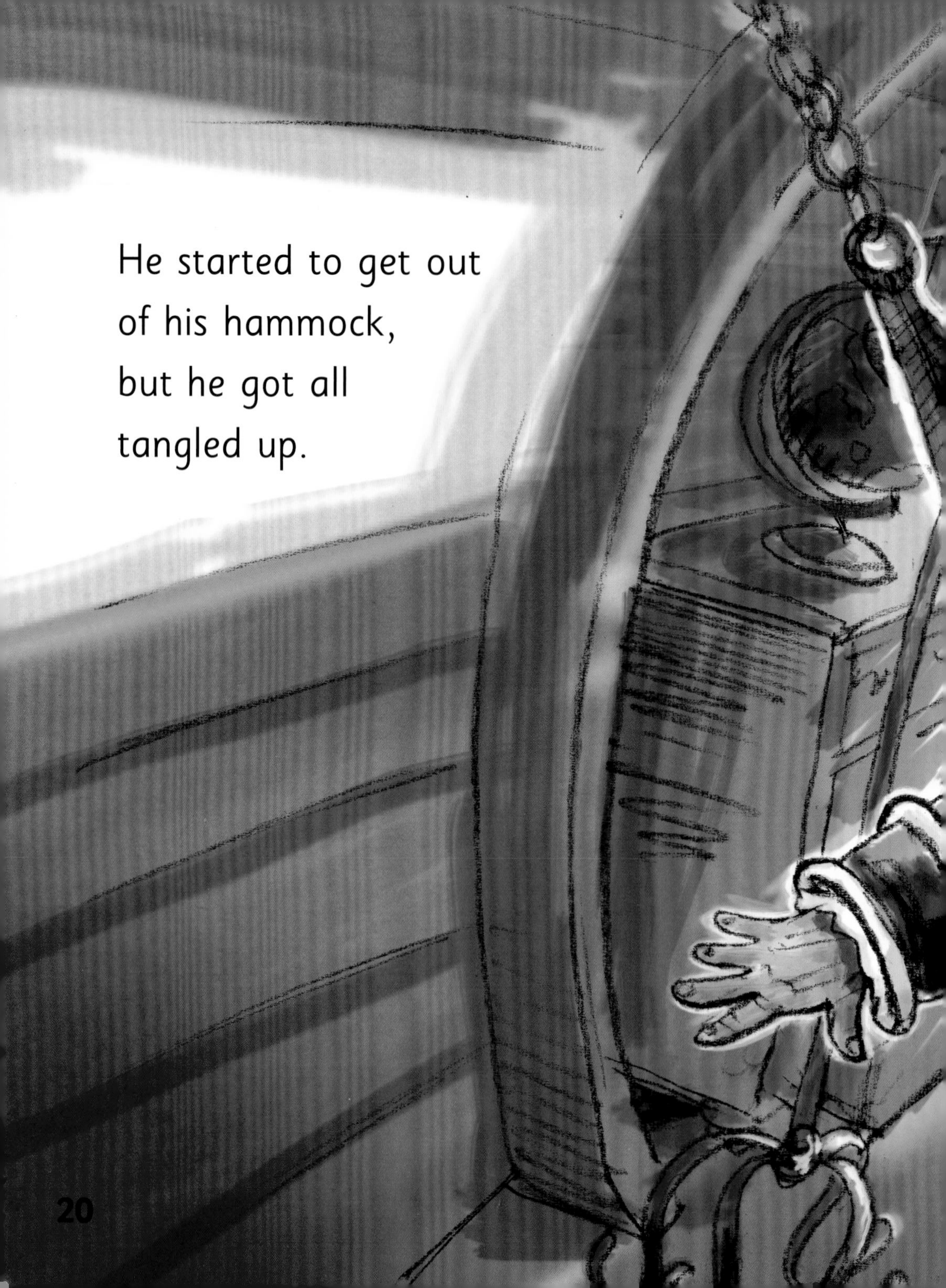

He started to get out
of his hammock,
but he got all
tangled up.

THUD! He landed on the floor.

A squashed, black, pirate hat landed on top of him.

Captain Red Beard had been lying on it!

“Well,” he smiled. “I’ve found my own hat, so it’s a hat full of gold for me!”

Think About!
Did the Captain really lose his hat?
Why is the Captain's hat so important to him?
Have you ever lost something important?